www.hants.gov.uk/library

Tel: 0300 555 1387

Hampshire County Council | *Love* YOUR LIBRARY

Guinea pig destined for stardom!

Written by **Pip Jones**

Illustrated by **Adam Stower**

ff

Hampshire County Council

C016393112

For Ava and Ruby, and for the children of

Mission Grove Primary School,

who once named a guinea pig.

First published in 2017
by Faber & Faber Limited
Bloomsbury House, 74–77 Great Russell Street
London WC1B 3DA
Typeset by Faber & Faber Limited
Printed and bound in the UK by CPI Group UK (Ltd)
Croydon CRO 4YY

All rights reserved

Text © Pip Jones
Illustrations © Adam Stower
The right of Pip Jones and Adam Stower to be identified as author and illustrator of this
work respectively has been asserted in accordance with Section 77 of the Copyright,
Designs and Patents Act 1988

This book is sold subject to the condition that it shall not, by way of trade or otherwise,
be lent, resold, hired out or otherwise circulated without the publisher's prior consent
in any form of binding or cover other than that in which it is published and without a
similar condition including this condition being imposed on the subsequent purchaser

A CIP record for this book is available
from the British Library
ISBN 978-0-571- 32754-6

FSC
www.fsc.org
MIX
Paper from
responsible sources
FSC® C101712

1 3 5 7 9 10 8 6 4 2

Meet Piggy Handsome!

Just look at that smile!

This guinea pig has such charisma and style!

He is, after all, the nineteenth generation

of Handsomes, and each one an utter sensation!

But poor Piggy Handsome, something went wrong.

He's been waiting for fame and for fortune SO long.

And now, here he sits, just dreaming up capers

(ways that he might get his name in the papers).

Could this be his chance? Are you desperate to know?

Well, let's see! Turn the page! And on with the show!

1

Tantrumptious!
or The woes of a pompous guinea pig

In a very ordinary house, in a mostly ordinary town called Gibblesby-on-Sea, a rather extraordinary guinea pig was stomping around his cage, hitting himself on the head with a rolled-up newspaper.

Ooh, not that you'd want to call it that actually.

I don't mean you wouldn't want to call the newspaper a *newspaper*. I mean, you wouldn't want to call the cage a *cage*. Good gracious, no! Not if Piggy Handsome was listening. He'd go mad.

'A cage?' he'd scream, his ginger fur standing on end to show quite how indignant he was. 'How DARE you! I've never been so insulted in *all my life* . . .'

And then he'd ramble on for a while about how he *actually* lived in a maisonette (which is a posh word for a flat with stairs). Then he'd show you his four-poster bed (which he'd fashioned out of the shredded paper that normal guinea pigs were expected to sleep in), and his en-suite bathroom (complete with a pink plastic toilet and a sink with gold taps). And *then* he'd insist you admire all the portraits of his very grand and extremely famous ancestors.

Well, those grand and extremely famous ancestors just happened to be the reason why Piggy Handsome was crashing around like a furious, fuming furball.

'Arrrrgh!' he yelled, whacking himself in the noggin again. 'Jeffry, my dear friend! What shall I *do*?'

High above Handsome, in an ornate birdcage, Jeff Budgie was trying to enjoy his morning snooze.

'What shall you do about *what*?' he yawned, peeking out from beneath his blue and black wing.

'About THIS THING!'

Piggy Handsome slapped his newspaper on to the floor, then jumped up and down on it until his pointy, piggy little feet had completely shredded the front page. Then he swooned, and collapsed into his armchair with a flop so flopsome that his beautifully styled quiff went flat.

After a moment – or rather, 'a dramatic pause'

– Piggy Handsome was bored with not talking.

'I'm nearly THREE!' he wailed. 'And NO ONE knows who I am! I'm not on the telly. I've *never* had my name in the newspaper. It's *humiliating*, Jeffry! I'm not . . . I'm not even . . .' Piggy Handsome sobbed dramatically, '*AN INTERNET SENSATION!*'

Now, you might be thinking: 'What's his problem? He's only three! He's got *loads* of time to fulfil his life ambitions.'

But actually, in guinea-pig years, being nearly three meant that Piggy Handsome was already nearly thirty years old. Practically an antique!

Not good. Not good *at all*. Especially since one of his ancestors – Tiddly Handsome – had become famous at the age of six months for learning how to play Beethoven's Sixth Symphony on the piano . . . BACKWARDS.

Anyway, all of this Jeff knew very well.

'Not this again,' he groaned, in a voice that was surprisingly deep and raspy for a tiny budgie.

Oh, sure, Jeff did the high-pitched budgie song, to please the human who delivered seeds and grated apple every day. But whenever the human wasn't there, Jeff Budgie sounded like a forty-five-year-old taxi driver from east London.

'Listen, Handsome,' Jeff gruffle-huffed, expertly pinging open the door to his cage and fluttering out. 'The truth is that guinea pigs, as a rule, ain't always . . . all . . . that . . .'

'FAMOUS!' shrieked Piggy Handsome. 'Jeffry, I'm no *mere guinea pig*! I'm a *Handsome*. And Handsomes have *always* been famous. It's all right for you. Budgies do nothing! Budgies are useless! Not good at anything! Well, apart from being blue and—'

'Yes, yes,' Jeff said, rolling his eyes. 'And squawking. Although, officially, it's tweeting, not squawking.'

FLWAT! A large, floppy cabbage leaf hit Jeff on the side of the head.

'Stop talking!' Piggy Handsome yelled. 'There's work to do, so think! I simply *cannot* be the only Handsome in history to not be famous. I need a plan. It needs to be good, it needs to be . . . foolproof. Just look at what I have to live up to!'

Piggy Handsome, who considered himself far too important to use his finger to point at things, picked up his pointing stick (which was just a stick with a plastic pointy finger at the end) and pointed at the portraits that were hanging on the wall of his cage . . . ahem, er, maisonette.

'Missy Handsome – sailed the length of the Danube! Rocket Handsome – the first guinea pig in space! Rugged Handsome – ac-TOR on stage and on screen! Doctor Dave Handsome – saved the life of the Queen's corgi! Ransom Handsome, oh, er . . .'

Handsome was pointing at a framed but tattered newspaper clipping. It displayed a photo of a grimacing, handcuffed guinea pig, and a headline that read: **No Ransom for Handsome: Gangster guinea pig captured by cops.**

'No, er, maybe not him . . .' Piggy Handsome muttered, quickly moving on to the next frame. 'But let's not forget Bella Handsome, a beauty beyond compare . . . !'

Jeff rolled his eyes (again). He'd heard it all before. Nibbling on some seeds, he spat the husks – PHWOOT! PHWOOT! – on to the floor and waited for Handsome to get to the bit about . . .

'Dear old Granny Handsome, who invented *claws*! Imagine that! How must the world have *been* before claws? Without claws, you would not be perching there, my feathered friend. And flying?

12

Well, each time you tried to land, you'd splat down *flat* on your beaky, blue face! Ha! Imagine life with no claws, Jeffry! Can you imagine it? *Can you?*"

Jeff finished his mouthful of millet seed, then cleared his throat.

'I'm afraid,' Jeff said slowly and clearly, 'you're a bit mixed up. Granny Handsome did NOT invent claws.'

Handsome didn't like that one bit. Granny Handsome was his favourite. His fur bristled. One eye twitched.

'Granny Handsome,' Jeff continued, '*claimed*

she'd invented a thing she liked to call "clawfs".
Only, for someone not quite so posh as what she
was – or not quite so posh as what you are, for that
matter – "clawfs" might be pronounced as . . .'

Jeff paused.

'As what?' Handsome demanded.

'Cloths,' Jeff said. 'Cloths. Them things what
you wipe mess up with.'

'Yes, of course! Clawfs!' Piggy Handsome
exclaimed, puffing with pride. 'Indeed, indeed!
Dear, ingenious Granny Handsome and her
amazing clawfs . . . !'

Jeff interrupted him.

'But actually,' Jeff said, 'Granny Handsome didn't invent cloths either.'

'What? Of course she did! Outrageous!' Handsome spluttered.

'Handsome, cloths were *actually* invented by a not even very clever cave woman called NARG.'

It was true. Jeff knew a thing or two about history. He'd read all the history books on the shelf. He also knew that cave people's names were always SHOUTED, which is why the true inventor's name was NARG and not Narg.

Piggy Handsome was absolutely trembling with rage.

He looked crosser than a swatted wasp.

He looked like he might explode.

Jeff, calm as ever, grinned.

Well, he didn't grin – beaks are quite impossible

to grin with. But he did the budgie version of grinning, the thing all budgies do when they're happy and content – he hid one leg in his feathers.

'How dare you!' Piggy Handsome hissed. 'How *dare* you sully the good name of Handsome! You . . . you . . . PARSNIP! I've a jolly good mind to . . . Hey, where's your leg gone?'

'BREAKFAST TIME!'

That deafening roar meant the human was coming. The door handle was already turning.

'Eep!' Piggy Handsome shooed Jeff out of his maisonette.

'Tweet!' Jeff fluttered back to his cage and pinged the metal door closed behind him.

Just in time, too. It wouldn't do for humans to learn that their pets – not just cats, but *all* pets – actually come and go as they jolly well please, cages or no cages. If humans were ever to discover such a thing, the pets' free food would stop, that's for sure. No more 'freeding time'. Nope. Not a chance.

And then pets like Piggy Handsome and Jeff Budgie would either have to get jobs or become farmers. (Although, actually, none of this applies to fish. Fish can't come and go as they please. Fish are pretty much stuck exactly where they are the moment they become pet fish.)

Anyway, the huge human, with her feet ... and her legs ... and her big fat head, lolloped into the room holding some plastic dishes and water bottles.

'If you don't mind,' Piggy Handsome shouted up from his armchair, 'I'd very much like a medium-sized bowl of Swiss muesli, instead of all these wretched cabbage leaves you insist on bringing every morning.'

Unfortunately for Handsome, all the human heard (as you might expect) was: '*EepEepEepEep!*

EepEep EepEepEepEep!' And so . . .

'Good morning, Piggy PooPoo!' the human replied, as she flung a fresh cabbage leaf on to Handsome's feeding trough (oops, or rather *dining table*).

'Piggy *what*?' exclaimed Handsome. 'My name is Handsome, *as well you know*, and I'd very much appreciate it if you could treat my name with the respect it deserv—*Aarghftftppt.'*

Oh dear. The massive human hands grabbed and pinched Piggy Handsome's cheeks, then squidged them and wiggled them up and down ever so roughly. (If you have a great aunt you don't see very often, you'll probably know how unpleasant this feels.)

'*Arghtftppt!* Get off me, you *fiend*!' Handsome shrieked.

It was a good thing the human let go (in order to empty the pellets of poo from Handsome's loo), because she was about to get quite a nip.

Piggy Handsome glared at his fresh green cabbage leaf, then repeatedly huffed and tutted as the human replaced his and Jeff's water bottles.

Then, when everything was all nice and clean,

the human thump-thumped towards the door . . .
and was gone.

'I cannot go on!' Piggy Handsome howled. 'I
tell you, I've HAD IT!'

Jeff, quietly content, munched away on his
seeds and apple.

'I dunno what your problem is, matey,' he
said with his mouth full. 'I think it's all pretty nice
around here. Want some seeds?'

'Nice?' Handsome spluttered. 'There's nothing
nice about it. This life is an abomination! I know
I was destined for greater things, and so I hereby

22

declare . . . that if my face is not in the papers tomorrow, I will change my name and be . . . *a Handsome no more!*'

Frogswallop!
or The art of losing badly

Following his exhausting outburst, Piggy Handsome was having a little lie-down. He'd torn up his fresh cabbage leaf and placed a small piece over each eye.

Jeff prodded him with one wing. 'What will

you change your name to,' he asked, 'if you don't get your name in the papers tomorrow?'

'The whole *point*,' Piggy Handsome gabbled, 'is that it *mustn't* come to tha—'

'Piggy Big Bum?' Jeff suggested.

'PARDON?'

'What?' said Jeff innocently. 'What's wrong with Piggy WigSome? I thought it might work, you know, 'cos of that lovely big hair thing you've got.'

'Oh, yes, I see,' said Handsome, sitting up and fluffing his quiff in the mirror. 'Very helpful. Sorry, I thought you said something else.'

Jeff stuck one leg in his feathers.

I suppose you might say that Handsome and Jeff were unlikely friends, really.

Handsome was a very shouty sort of creature. He liked nothing more than stropping about, yelling insults and stamping on things. Jeff, on the other hand, was calm and quiet – the sort who did a great deal of eye-rolling and gentle teasing.

Yet, despite their differences, Handsome and Jeff *were* friends, and in that way they were living proof that opposites really do attract. Somehow they just went together, like a question and an answer.

Or night and day.

Or cheese and pickle.

'I know!' Jeff said suddenly, his eyes twinkling. 'How about a game of Froggy, down at the pond?

It'll help you to clear your head. And anyway, you're three games behind. I'll give you a chance to catch up.'

Aha! Oh yes, one thing Piggy Handsome and Jeff *did* have in common was a competitive streak.

They often quarrelled about what games to play, and they were good at different things – for example, Handsome was better at bowling, while Jeff was better at high jump (although it was impossible to tell whether he cheated, what with having wings and all that).

The human was constantly befuddled by the

abandoned leftovers of their larks – especially the
extremely sharp pencils (or 'javelins') sticking out
of the plump sofa.

'I am *not* three games behind,' Handsome blustered. 'The last game didn't count because the second lily pad on my side was a duff. It couldn't even hold my weight for a second!'

'All right,' Jeff chuckled. '*Two* games behind, but I get to go first. You ready?'

Piggy Handsome puffed out his chest. 'Of course I'm ready!'

Jeff peeped round the door, took a deep breath and said . . .

'BRRRRNNNG!   BRRRRNNNG! BRRRRNNNG!'

It's not just parrots who mimic noises, you know.

In the hall, their human thump-thumped towards the telephone and swiped up the receiver.

'Hello?' she said. 'HELLO? HELLO?'

Jeff winked at Piggy Handsome, who laughed from his little round belly.

'*Huphuphuphuphup!*'

He sounded like a piglet with hiccups.

It wasn't an easy thing to make Piggy Handsome laugh, because Piggy Handsome was always so worried about 'being a Handsome' and 'getting famous'. In fact, it's possible that Jeff Budgie was the only living creature who was actually able to do it.

While the human's back was turned, Handsome and Jeff strolled past, through the kitchen, and out of the back door.

*

The garden looked much like any other town garden. It had plant pots, a lawn with a cat poo on it, and a long winding path. A spider's web twinkled in the morning sunlight. A butterfly fluttered prettily past. A skittish bluebottle forgot to look where it was going, and flew right into the greenhouse door with a painful splat.

Right at the end of the garden was a pond surrounded by tall reeds. And on the other side of the pond was Banger, the very elderly sausage dog from number forty-three.

'A very good morning to you, Banger, my stretchy, stubby-legged friend,' Handsome said, slightly wearily.

'Wotcha, Banger!' chirped Jeff. 'Fancy being referee? We're having a game of Froggy!'

'Can't at the moment,' Banger replied. 'I'm concentrating on not sitting down.'

Both Piggy Handsome and Jeff looked confused. Banger's little legs were *so* little that she

already looked like she *was* sitting down. The rear part of her squidgy tummy was even touching the ground.

'Why are you concentrating on not sitting down?' Piggy Handsome asked.

'With these creaky legs, it'll take me forty-five minutes to get up again,' Banger said gravely. 'And I need to be able to *move*! At a moment's notice! Oh, you young things, with your bright eyes and your bouncy knee joints, you have no idea what it's like!'

'What it's like to be really, really, really, really, really, really old?' Jeff asked.

'*Huphuphuphuphup!*' Handsome giggled under his breath. 'Ssshh!'

'I'm ninety-two, you know! Or am I ninety-seven? Not sure. I think I slept through my last birthday. Or last two birthdays. Sorry, did you ask me something?'

Banger was, in fact, nearly a hundred and one years old – in dog years, that is – which is a very impressive age indeed for a sausage dog.

'Er . . . yes,' replied Jeff. 'We just wondered why you have to be able to move at a moment's notice. You usually don't move all day.'

'FredHead will come looking for me soon,' Banger replied in a low, whispery voice. 'He wants to take me back to that horrible Doctor VetHead. I know he does. I've seen the basket he puts me in! He thinks it's hidden under the kitchen table, but I remember a time when there *were* no squirrels in this garden! And don't get me started on vegetarian dog biscuits . . .'

Banger had a habit of beginning a story about one thing and then talking about fifteen other things without pausing for breath. Once, she'd talked to a mayfly for so long – about handbags, and Easter eggs, and the colours of cars, and space travel, and dandelions, and alligators, and garden spades, and cheese, and dust, and a mystical place called Scandinavia, and televisions, and coal, and snooker, and rhubarb, and donkey feet — that it had actually *died* while listening to her. It had just run out of life. Of course, mayflies do have a relatively short lifespan, but still.★

'And it's not even like I *wanted* to chew that sheepskin rug . . .' Banger continued.

'Yeah, right!' Jeff said. 'OK, we'll just be over here . . .'

★ No mayflies were hurt in the imagining of this story.

Banger babbled on, while Jeff and Piggy Handsome moved around the pond to find the perfect starting point for their game of Froggy.

It's unlikely that you will have played Froggy yourself – well, not the version of Froggy that Piggy Handsome and Jeff liked to play, anyway. The object of the game was to cross the water using the lily pads, shouting 'FROGGY!' as loudly as they could, and reach the other side before the very irritable toad who lived in the pond leaped out of the water and slapped them in the eye with his sticky tongue.

It wasn't as easy as it sounds.

'I'm starting here today,' Piggy Handsome said confidently, poking the closest lily pad with his toe to check it had some bounce.

But then he looked lost in thought again.

'What's up?' Jeff asked. 'Oh, all right, you can go first if you really want to.'

'It's not that,' Handsome huffed. 'It's just . . . I really thought that *someone* would have appreciated my speech yesterday at the Town Hall. I thought that *someone* would have agreed with my ideas about allowing rodents to become politicians, that *someone* would have taken my picture for the *Gibblesby Herald*.'

'Maybe if you hadn't been talking at the same time as the Mayor was giving *her* speech . . .' Jeff suggested.

'It's too late to tell me that now!' said Handsome. 'Anyway, how is this going to help clear my head?' he demanded. 'How will I ever have another such stupendous idea for getting famous? I don't WANT to have to change my name to Piggy WigSome! I need to think! I can't just pretend everything is all right and stay out here playing FROGGY . . .!'

SWIIIITTTTT!

'OUCH!'

The toad who had slapped Handsome in the eye with his sticky tongue croaked 'Bog off!' and then plopped back under the water.

'Cor, he got you good and proper!' Jeff chuckled. 'Is that another point to me?'

'It didn't count!' Piggy Handsome shrieked, storming back towards the house. 'Are you coming or not?'

Jeff rolled his eyes.

'I'm coming,' he replied. 'Oh, and see ya, Banger. Good luck with Doctor VetHead.'

★

While Jeff fluttered after Piggy Handsome, Banger began chatting to a woodlouse sitting on the wall at the end of the garden.

There was nothing particularly interesting about the woodlouse, and there was nothing particularly interesting about the wall.

But *beyond* the wall, and beyond the garden that lay beyond the wall, and beyond the house that lay beyond the garden that lay beyond the wall . . .

Well, put it this way: three streets away, in a grim-looking building with murky windows, something interesting most certainly *was* going on.

Dumbvillainry!
or That growing sense of Gloom...

Gloom Street had not always been called Gloom Street. Once upon a time, the sign at the top of the road had actually read 'Bloom Street'.

But, maybe because the sun hardly ever managed to shine through the thick, twisted branches of the ancient oak trees, somebody had crossed out the 'B' and painted a 'G' there instead. And maybe because there were no roses or buttercups or forget-me-nots – only mud and stinging nettles – no one had ever bothered changing it back.

Anyway, behind the battered old door of number sixty-six Gloom Street, an odd-looking pair of humans were dunking biscuits into mugs of milky tea.

Dan and Dolly Dixon were twins – although you might not have guessed as much. Dan was short, with matted blond hair, a round face and a snotty snub nose. Dolly was tall and thin, with long, dark curls and a wide, crooked smile.

'You're 'orrible!' Dolly shouted.

'You're terrible!' Dan yelled back.

'Ain't it brilliant!' they both roared at once.

Dan grabbed another pile of chocolate digestives and shoved them all in his mouth.

Dolly copied him.

'So this is the plan,' Dan said, spitting biscuit crumbs over the table. 'We'll burst into Jones's Jewellery Shop at 10 a.m. We'll grab all the cash and diamonds, then we'll steal a car and we'll make our getaway.'

'Then we'll move to a huge mansion in the country,' Dolly added, spitting even more crumbs over the table, her blue eyes twinkling with greed. 'And I'll wear all the gems, and we'll tell everyone we're the Royal Family. And we'll get servants and make 'em scrub our feet for us.'

Dolly wiggled her warty toes, scraping her long, yellow toenails on the floor.

'Easy as pie!' Dan cried. 'Our new life awaits us, hoorah! Aint it 'orrible, I mean brilliant, yeah!'

4

KungFulery!
or How to (sort of) defeat a cranky cat

Piggy Handsome and Jeff Budgie made their way back to the room they shared (Handsome liked to call it the West Wing of the house), with its big bay window and its bulging bookshelves.

While Handsome was fluffing his quiff and

rambling on about the ways he might get famous, and while Jeff was quietly muttering about how he now *definitely* had a three-point lead in Froggy, they didn't notice the door creak open behind them.

They didn't notice that their *enemy* had silently entered the room and was now watching them both from high above on the desk.

An enemy with dagger teeth and razor claws.

An enemy with a glare like glass.

An enemy who *stank* like, like . . . Marmite and evil combined.

'*Miaow-rrll*.'

'UH–OH!' Jeff wasted no time in fluttering back to his cage.

Like a flash, Piggy Handsome darted into his walk-in wardrobe and slammed the door.

You'll probably assume that Handsome had gone into the wardrobe to hide. Indeed, for any other guinea pig suddenly finding itself in the company of a manky, sly cat like Cranky Scrapper, hiding in a wardrobe would be a very sensible thing to do.

But Jeff (who *was* sensibly far out of reach) knew that what was actually about to happen was . . .

'*Haaw-WAH!*'

Handsome, now dressed head to toe in black, kicked the wardrobe door open with a wallop.

'Cranky Scrapper!' Handsome declared loudly, with his paws aloft. 'You villainous feline! Fancy an extra meal, eh? Or have you just come to taunt us with your evil?'

Cranky sighed.

She inspected her claws.

Then replied, 'Bored.'

Cranky always popped by the West Wing when she was bored. She had no intention of eating Piggy Handsome, or Jeff for that matter. She was far too well fed by the human to bother.

Handsome glanced over at Jeff. 'Fear not, fluttery friend,' he whispered. 'I'll use just a few moves I learned from my great uncle, Chan Zen Handsome.'

'Ah yes!' Cranky laughed. 'Chan Zen Handsome. Another one of your famous ancestors! It's a shame you'll never amount to anything *yourself*, isn't it, *little Piggy* . . . with your bad hair and your big bottom.'

All the fur on Piggy Handsome's back bristled furiously. 'How *DARE* you . . .' he began. 'I'll . . .

I'm going to . . . I'll teach you a thing or two about Handsomes! All Handsomes! Including *me*! *WATCH AND LEARN*!'

It was hard to watch, though.

I don't mean it was hard to *see* on account of Piggy Handsome moving so fast that he became some sort of heroic kung fu blur.

No, I really do mean it was hard to *watch* – because whatever Handsome was doing, it most certainly was NOT kung fu.

First there was a cartwheel, then a roly-poly and a couple of star jumps. Then Handsome

did a strange hip-wiggle thing, during which he accidentally knocked his water bottle off its wire. Then he dropped down and bounced on his bum, before doing a side roll to the left, then to the right, then . . .

Several minutes later, with a dramatic flapping arm motion, accompanied by a loud '*HYAAAA-AWWW!*', Handsome *finally* reached the leg of the writing desk.

He stood out of breath, his chest heaving, glaring up at Cranky Scrapper.

Cranky returned Handsome's stare with

slanted green eyes. She slowly licked her front paw, being sure to stretch her claws out nice and wide.

Jeff shuddered, but Handsome stood his ground.

'I think it was time you were going, Cranky, don't you?' he said confidently.

Cranky Scrapper gave a long sigh. 'No,' she huskily replied.

Handsome was just trying to decide his next move when a strange *CCHHHPT* noise came from above him.

Cranky smiled menacingly.

'Huh?' Handsome said. High above him, the corner of something square came into view.

CCHHHPT.

Using her paw, Cranky Scrapper pushed the thing again. It was a book – a very large, very heavy book. And nearly half of it was now over the edge of the desk, right above Handsome's head.

'Don't you DARE!' Handsome said.

CCHHPT.

Cranky nudged the book again, ever closer to the edge.

'I'm *warning* you, Cranky, if you—'

CCHHPT.

'I mean it. If you push that thing ONE more time—'

CCHHPT.

'Er, Handsome,' Jeff said, 'you might just want to step away from there, mate . . .'

'I'll do no such thing! I absolutely refuse to—'

CCHHPT.

'CRANKY, I'M WARNING YOU—'

CHPT.

It took the tiniest of nudges to finish the job.

The book began to fall.

As the book fell, it twisted, its covers opened and its pages splayed, fluttering in the air.

Handsome lifted his arms and did some sort of move — well, if he'd been in a swimming pool, it probably would have been backstroke — in an attempt to deflect the massive, plummeting book.

But he failed.

The book kept falling in his direction.

And it landed ...

'*GHUMPFT!*'

... over Piggy Handsome with a thud.

Yes 'over', not 'on top of'.

By some amazing stroke of luck, the enormous book had landed on the edges of its hard cover, making a perfect triangle over Handsome.

'HA!' came his muffled voice, the instant he realised he wasn't squashed even a little bit. 'Nice try, Cranky! You hadn't counted on my lightning reflexes, which must have—*HARGMPFT!*'

Cranky Scrapper pounced down from the desk, landing like an Olympic gymnast on the book's spine, squashing Piggy Handsome underneath.

'Bye for now,' Cranky taunted, as she stepped off the book and headed for the door. Her scraggy tail flicked as she slunk through the gap and was gone.

'Handsome?' Jeff called, pinging open his cage

and swooping down to the ground. 'Handsome? Handsome? Can you hear me, pal? Handsome? Are you all right? Handsome? Oh, *Handsome*!'

Silence.

. . . .

. . . .

. . . .

. . . .

No, sorry. Not silence. I mean 'dramatic pause'. Because, suddenly, from the depths of those pages . . .

'Waban extrorbnarik! Ist eeely ite . . .'

'What's that?' Jeff said. 'Can't hear you with that book on your head. Oh, hang on.'

Jeff grabbed the spine of the book with his hooked beak and, flapping with all his might, heaved it up just enough for Piggy Handsome to crawl out.

'I *said*,' Handsome puffed, 'what an *extraordinary* book. It's really quite fascinating. And do you know . . . Yes, I think it's given me an *idea*.'

'An idea, Handsome?'

'Yes! An idea! I think I've got it, Jeffry. *I know how I'm going to get famous!*'

5

Stick'em^{up}down^{up}down^{up}...!

or The worst stick-up ever

Mr Jones, a round and cheery human with thick white eyebrows and a shiny pink face, was polishing an emerald ring when ...

DING-A-NING!

... the bell on the door to his jewellery shop

told him he had his first customer of the day.

'Good morning!' Mr Jones beamed, placing the ring on the glass counter and looking up over the rim of his silver glasses. 'And how can I help you this fine morni . . .'

The customers didn't look very friendly.

They were both wearing black eye masks.

The short one was carrying a big grey sack.

The tall one yelled, 'It's a good morning for *US*! Not for you! Put your hands up!'

'Oh!' Mr Jones cried, putting his hands up, just as he'd been told.

'Now gives us all yer jewels!' demanded the short one.

Mr Jones picked up a tray lined with rings.

'Put yer hands up, I said!' shrieked the tall one.

Mr Jones put the tray down, so he could put his hands up again.

'Oi!' shouted the short one. 'I told you to give us yer jewels!'

'Er . . .' Mr Jones picked up the tray again.

'HANDS UP!'

'GIVE US YER JEWELS!'

'HANDS UP!'

'GIVE US YER JEWELS!'

'HANDS UP!'

'GIVE US YER JEWELS!'

Well, poor Mr Jones. He was beginning to look more like he was dancing than being robbed by (well, you know who they were) Dan and Dolly Dixon.

'Which do you want me to do?' Mr Jones sighed.

Dan whispered to Dolly. 'He can't have his hands up *and* put all the jewels in the bag, can he?'

'Which is more important?' Dolly replied. 'You can't do a stick-up without making someone put their hands up, can you?'

'How about we make him put *one* hand up, and he uses the other hand to put the loot in the sack?' Dan suggested.

Dan and Dolly's conversation was taking so long that Mr Jones decided to nip out the back to get his packet of Custard Creams. He'd already eaten two of them when Dolly finally shouted, 'Good plan! Stick *ONE* hand up . . . Hang on, are you left-handed or right-handed?'

'Who, me?' Mr Jones asked, looking up from his crossword. 'I'm right-handed.'

'So stick your left hand up,' Dolly instructed. 'And use your right hand to fill this sack with all yer . . .'

'BISCUITS!' Dan yelled.

'*Biscuits?* We want his jewels, banana-brain!' Dolly tutted.

'Oh yeah!' said Dan. 'Ain't it brilliant!'

'Yeah!' said Dolly.

Mr Jones pushed his glasses up his nose and squinted a little.

'Hang on, you're holding a . . . That's a stick of rock, isn't it?'

He was right. The thing that Dolly was pointing at Mr Jones was a large, pink-and-yellow candy cane.

'Yeah, but, but . . .' Dan spluttered, 'it's an, er . . . EXPLODING stick of rock! So hand over the loot! And the biscuits!'

'Oh dear, righto.' Mr Jones dropped the packet of Custard Creams into the sack, then began tipping in all the rings, necklaces and bracelets. Then he took the wads of ten, twenty and fifty pound notes from the till and put those in as well.

As the terrible thieves ran down the road, cackling like crazy hyenas, Mr Jones picked up the phone and, as you'd expect, he jolly well called the police.

Hulathoughtit!
or A very nearly good idea

The cover of the enormous book that had squashed

Piggy Handsome was shiny, and silver, and hard,

and square, and pointy at the corners, and ...Well,

let's just say it was full of promise. In large red letters,

the title read: *The Big Book of Brilliant World Records!*

Piggy Handsome ran his hand over the spine.

'This is it, Jeffry!' he whispered. 'I'm going to break a World Record! I'll be *sensational*. I'll be in all the newspapers. Ooh! I might get a slot on Gibblesby TV News! The question is: which world record should I break?'

Handsome stood there for a moment.

Pondering.

Tapping his chin.

'Maybe we should have a look in—' Jeff began.

'Ssshh!'

'We could open the b—'

'Ssshh!'

'I just thought if we—'

'*Do be quiet, Jeffry!* I think we should open the book and get some ideas. Help me turn it over.'

Jeff rolled his eyes and then helped Piggy Handsome heave *The Big Book of Brilliant World Records!* so the pages were facing upwards, all white and crisp and ready to read.

'Right! We must get started *immediately*!' Piggy Handsome blustered, clapping his paws in excitement. 'I'll go and put on my Reading Jacket.'

Oh yes, his Reading Jacket.

You see, Piggy Handsome felt it was terribly important to wear the right type of clothing for every occasion and activity – and that's something you'll probably understand, *up to a point.*

I mean, I expect you have a swimming costume? Or football boots? Or a party outfit?

Well, as well as his Reading Jacket, Piggy Handsome had a Stirring Smock. It had a picture of a spoon on it (which he said reminded him to keep stirring) and he wore it whenever he was stirring things, which wasn't all that often really.

Handsome got much more use out of his

Shouting Hat, which was red and pointy and had two earplugs attached, to protect his ears from his own shouting.

Oh yes, he used his Shouting Hat *at least* three times a week, when he spent an hour or so on the windowsill, shouting at whatever happened to be passing – like the postman, or a magpie, or, well, anything really.

'HELLO! DO YOU KNOW WHO I AM?'

he'd shout. 'I'M PIGGY HANDSOME! YES, REALLY! HEY, YOU THERE! YOU'RE NOT VERY GOOD AT FLYING, ARE YOU, FOR A BIRD? I CAN SPEAK FRENCH, YOU KNOW! OOH LAA LAA, LA FRANCE! HEY, LOOK AT MY TOENAILS!'

Anyway, with his Reading Jacket nicely buttoned, Piggy Handsome leaned over the book. Jeff used a wing to turn the pages while Handsome peered at all the photos of Brilliant World Records and the words underneath describing what had been done.

'Now, let's see . . .' Handsome said. 'The shortest ever worm. The longest worm to get lost down a hole. The largest peanut swallowed whole. The largest hole made by a peanut fired from a bicycle pump, which was aimed at a blancmange. The longest time taken to build a sausage . . .'

'Build a *sausage*?' Jeff said, leaning down to look.

'Oh no, wait,' Piggy Handsome smoothed out a fold in the page. 'It's actually the longest time taken to build a ship out of shells, and then, erm . . . the shortest sausage it took to sink a ship.'

'Hey, Handsome, what about this section?'

Jeff blurted, wide-eyed. 'Brilliant *Death-Defying World Records*! Now *that's* how to get on telly.'

Jeff pointed at a picture of a human who'd tied his shoelaces together, handcuffed himself, strapped himself to a rocket (probably not in that order, thinking about it) and was standing next to a small gap on one of the largest ice sheets of the

South Pole, aiming himself at the freezing water.

'Ooh! Hula-hooping!' Piggy Handsome exclaimed, having hurriedly flicked on a few pages. 'Wait here!'

With that, Piggy Handsome dashed to the door. After checking the coast was clear, he marched out of the West Wing, and made his way up the stairs.

Handsome knew the East Wing (the rest of the house) very well. He'd spent many an enjoyable afternoon strolling around, rifling through the human's drawers, and so on.

Moments later, he burst back through the door

with a 'Ta-da!'. Then, from behind his back, he pulled out a shiny golden bangle. The diamonds that were encrusted all the way around the edge glittered in the sunlight.

'Cor, that looks expensive,' Jeff said, giving one of the diamonds a hard peck to check it was real.

'Oh, it wasn't expensive *at all*!' Piggy Handsome laughed. 'It was completely free, as it happens. I found it lying around upstairs. And it makes a perfect hula hoop. Watch.'

Piggy Handsome stepped through the hoop, and tried to pull it up to his waist – it stopped short, however, when it arrived in the area of his bottom.

'Ahem,' Handsome mumbled after two or three unsuccessful tugs. 'You know, I think it must be one of those "over-the-head" hula hoops. Modern design.'

With the hula hoop primed and ready around his middle, Piggy Handsome took a deep breath and . . .

HWISH . . . HWISH . . . HWISH . . . HWISH . . . HWISH . . . HWISH . . .

'I'm hula-hooping!' Handsome yelled. 'See? Check the clock for my start time! How do I look?'

Imagine a guinea pig hula-hooping.

How would it look?

Yes, exactly. It looked *hilarious*.

If it hadn't been for Handsome's tiny little head, he would have looked like a planet. One of the ones with a ring around it, like Saturn or Neptune, except fluffy.

Well, Jeff Budgie made a point of only making fun of Piggy Handsome in a way that wouldn't hurt his feelings (or in a way he wouldn't notice), so he replied, 'Yup. Looking gooooooooood . . .'

HWISH . . . HWISH . . . HWISH . . . HWISH . . . HWISH . . .

'Thought so!' Handsome puffed. 'Now check

the book. How long do I have to do this for,

to break the Brilliant World Record?'

'Erm . . .' Jeff said, examining the page. 'Let me see . . . Yes, the Brilliant World Record for hula-hooping is seventy-four hours, fifty-four minutes and nine seconds.'

'Right!' Handsome said (the hula hoop visibly slowing down a bit).

HWISH . . . . . . HWISH . . . . . HWISH . . . . . . HWISH . . . . . .

'And how long have I been doing it so far?'

Jeff glanced at the clock. 'Fourteen seconds,' he replied.

'WHAT? Are you sure?'

'Fifteen now.'

'Is that all? Really?'

'Sixteen now.'

'SECONDS? I'm not . . . sure I . . .' Piggy Handsome's cheeks were going a pretty shade of crimson, and his quiff was beginning to glisten with sweat. 'It's really . . . quite hard work . . .'

HWISH . . . . . . HWISH . . . . . .HWISH . . . . . .

'You can do it! Only seventy-four hours, fifty-three minutes and forty-six seconds to go now!' Jeff shouted encouragingly. 'Oh, although . . .'

Jeff was leaning over the page in front of him again, and reading some very small words under a headline that said: 'Rules.'

'Although what?' Piggy Handsome gasped. 'What is it?'

'Ah, erm. Actually, Handsome,' Jeff replied, 'it don't count.'

'WHAT?' Piggy Handsome shrieked. He tossed the hula hoop to the ground, got his breath back a bit and staggered over to Jeff.

'*You made me hula hoop,*' Handsome seethed, 'for TWENTY-FIVE SECONDS AND IT

DOESN'T COUNT?'

Jeff shrugged, as well he might.

Because, of course, Jeff hadn't *made* Piggy Handsome do anything at all. And when Piggy Handsome had decided he wanted to break a Brilliant World Record for hula-hooping, he might have thought to check the rules himself.

If he had done, he would have seen that:

All Brilliant World Record attempts must be prearranged with the Brilliant World Records Association.

And also:

All Brilliant World Record attempts must be attended

by an Official Brilliant World Record Association Judge,
who will witness and verify that a Brilliant World Record
has indeed been either set or broken. Any claims of Brilliant
World Records will be dismissed unless these rules have been
abided by in full.

Nope. It definitely didn't count. And Piggy Handsome was *livid*.

With his fists curled up in furious little balls, and with one eye twitching, he stomped back to the hula hoop, and swiped it off the ground.

Then he climbed up to the windowsill and flung open the window.

'Oh . . . PELLETS!' he shouted, tossing the hula hoop (or rather, extremely valuable diamond-encrusted gold bangle) high into the air. A magpie promptly swooped down and snatched it, before flying away, cawing triumphantly.

Piggy Handsome sighed and, with his head hanging, he just let himself sort of drip off the windowsill into a sad little puddle on the floor.

All the huff-puff had gone out of him.

He looked like a popped balloon.

Or a deflated soufflé.

'To be perfectly honest, Handsome,' Jeff said quietly, 'when you think about it, I'm not sure how that hula-hooping would've got you famous. I mean, the whole point of doing something to get famous is that other people see you doing it. How would anyone have *known* you'd hula-hooped for three days without stopping?'

'Ohhhhhh,' Piggy Handsome sighed, pointing absent-mindedly at the radio on the desk. 'I thought I'd just be able to ring them on that speaker thing, and tell them I'd done it, and then they'd send round the newspaper reporters, and the photographers, and the people from . . .'

Handsome sobbed (although it sounded more like a goose honk).

'. . . *Gibblesby TV News!* And now all is lost. I will not be famous by tomorrow. And, alas, a Handsome always stands by his word. I will have to change my name to Piggy WigSome.'

Jeff Budgie suddenly felt a bit bad about that.

'Fancy a game of darts?' he chirped. 'Might cheer you up. I saw some cocktail sticks around here somewhere. We could chuck 'em at that.'

Jeff pointed hopefully at an antique clock on the mantelpiece.

'No, thank you,' Piggy Handsome replied weakly. 'I'm rather woozy. I feel like I might faint. Fan me, would you? Hurry.'

Jeff looked around the room for something he could use as a fan. He couldn't use Handsome's cabbage leaf, as it'd been ripped up to make refreshing eye patches. Jeff thought he might be able to pull out a page from *The Big Book of Brilliant World Records*, but he worried it might, you know, tip Handsome over the edge.

In Handsome's cage, the morning newspaper was still crumpled on the floor.

'That ought to do it!' Jeff said, hopping over.

He pulled away the front page that Handsome had shredded during his early-morning tantrum, and he was about to fold the rest of the paper into a fan shape when suddenly . . .

'I don't believe it!' Jeffry exclaimed.

Piggy Handsome's ears pricked. It was very unlike Jeff Budgie to be excited about *anything*.

'You don't believe what?' Handsome asked. 'What is it?'

'Well, this really is a stroke of luck,' Jeff said, with his wings on his hips, marvelling at whatever it was he was looking at in the newspaper.

'What's a stroke of luck?'

'It's unbelievable!'

'*What*'s unbelievable?' Piggy Handsome was on his feet now.

'Well, well, well. Of *all* the days this could happen . . .' Jeff was shaking his head in disbelief, at whatever unbelievable thing it was that he couldn't believe.

'OF ALL THE DAYS *WHAT* COULD HAPPEN?' Piggy Handsome's voice had gone very high and squeaky. He sounded like a kettle at near boiling point. 'Jeff Budgie, if you don't tell me what you're talking about RIGHT NOW, I will—'

'Look!' Jeff picked up the newspaper and held it up so Handsome could read the thick black words:

Want to be a Brilliant World Record Breaker? Today is YOUR chance!

and underneath . . .

Gibblesby-on-Sea will be under the spotlight this afternoon, as the Brilliant

World Record Chip Chomping Championship is set to take place at 2 p.m. on the seafront.

An Official Brilliant World Record Association Judge will watch as hopefuls line up to take on the current Brilliant World Record holder Charlie 'The Chops' Fryer.

Competitor places are still available.

Spectators are advised that large crowds are expected . . .

. . . and Gibblesby TV News will be reporting.

7

Booteaousness!

or Looking good in a runaway roller boot

'*Gibblesby TV News!* QUICK! We have *no time to lose!*'

Piggy Handsome yelled, as he ran into his walk-in

wardrobe and slammed the door.

Over the strange noises of Handsome trying

on various outfits – *Hfft! Euhmp! Bing! Ouch!*

Uuuuhhhhfft! Eeeeee! — Jeff managed to have a snooze.

Then he woke up, had a good stretch, and preened his chest feathers for a while. Then he went and plucked the strings of the guitar that was propped up in the corner of the room. He'd almost learned how to play a song called 'Why Are We Waiting?' when finally . . .

'I'm READY!'

The wardrobe doors swung open. Piggy Handsome was wearing a golden cape that had the word 'CHAMP' embroidered on the back. With

his hands on his hips, he tried to flex his tiny chest muscles. His quiff was standing straight up – a shiny, stiff triangle.

'Shall we go then?' Jeff asked. 'We've got just over an hour to—'

'Stop dawdling – let's go!'

Piggy Handsome had already dashed out of the room into the hall, his cape billowing. Jeff hopped out behind him.

Handsome scrambled up on to a table near the front door. He swiped a bunch of keys (which was as heavy as a bunch of keys any jailer might own) and tossed them down towards Jeff, shouting, 'Catch!'

The keys landed with a blood-jangling thud two millimetres from where Jeff stood.

'They could've killed me,' he said drily.

'Don't be such a baby, Jeffry!' Handsome replied, leaping down and grabbing the keys. 'Follow me. We'll take the car!'

★

Piggy Handsome pressed the button on the fat, black car key.

BLOOP! The car's indicator lights flashed, and

the doors unlocked.

'Handsome?' Jeff said. 'You do know that you can't—*Hrmmph!*'

Piggy Handsome had used Jeff's beak to hoist himself up on to a tall pile of boxes. He climbed up to the top, then yanked at the door handle. Jeff fluttered up and perched on the wing mirror.

'Handsome, you can't take the car,' Jeff sighed.

'Why on earth not?' Handsome asked. 'It'd take us six hours to walk to the seafront. And the Chip Chomping Championship starts in only ONE hour. We'd be . . . ummmm . . .'

Handsome tried to do a quick sum.

'We'd be *terribly* late!'

'Yes, taking the car is a good plan *in theory*,' Jeff said, 'but it's a plan with a major flaw.'

'Which *is*?' Handsome huffed as he hopped into the car and dropped completely out of view.

'Which *is* that you can't drive.'

Jeff leaned down and peered through the window.

Handsome bounced up and down, trying to grab the steering wheel. 'I *definitely* can, Jeffry. Give me a moment . . . I . . . just . . . need . . .

to . . . reach . . .'

Jeff rolled his eyes.

A few minutes later, Piggy Handsome had to have a little sit-down.

'Are you *sure* I can't drive, Jeffry?' he puffed. 'I could have *sworn* I've driven this thing before.'

'You definitely ain't.' Jeff shook his head.

'THEN I AM DOOMED!' Piggy Handsome wailed, throwing the bunch of keys on to the floor. In his temper, he kicked the handbrake hard. It popped and released with a CLUNK! The car slowly rolled forwards, and squashed a lawnmower in front of it with a grinding crunch.

'Take that, you big, stupid, massive *car face*!' Handsome shrieked.

Jeff might have tried to calm Piggy Handsome's riotous ranting, but he'd spotted something interesting poking out of the top of a box. He flitted over to it, and tugged with his beak.

Out toppled a blue roller boot, complete with shiny black wheels, long red laces and a silver zigzag down the side.

'Hmm. Yeah, this ought to do it.' Jeff pulled the roller boot upright. Next, he used his beak to tie the laces together at the front. Then he secured them around his chest like a harness and checked his wings could flap freely.

'Handsome!' Jeff called. 'Come on, pal. We're sorted. Let's go!'

DZZZZZZZ. The car window lowered.

Piggy Handsome hauled himself up the side of the door and peeped out. His eyes lit up when he saw Jeff.

'A chauffeured *boot*! Oh, Jeffry!' Handsome cried. 'Yes, yes! You shall be my shoe-ffeaur!'

Handsome leaped into the roller boot and made himself comfy.

'Absolute *genius*,' he marvelled. 'I'm really rather surprised I didn't think of it myself.'

Jeff rolled his eyes while Handsome grabbed a spanner from a toolbox on the floor and threw it, very hard, at a large switch on the wall.

'Bullseye!' Jeff shouted.

The electric garage door clicked and slowly began to rise. Jeff blinked at the bright sunlight streaming in. Piggy Handsome pulled a pair of black sunglasses from a fold in his cape and put them on.

'Drive, Jeffry!' Handsome commanded. 'We're going to the seafront!'

★

Flying perilously low to the ground and with Piggy Handsome, in the roller boot, racing along behind him, Jeff shot out from the garage, down the drive,

and to the end of Elms Avenue.

'EEEEEEP!' Handsome screamed as they rounded a corner. They joined the main road, which was buzzing with noisy engines and enormous black wheels. 'Jeffry! Are you *sure* this thing is safe? You're going *terribly fast*!'

Piggy Handsome held on to his shades as they screeched around a bend and narrowly missed crashing into a huge motorcycle.

'I only got two speeds, Handsome!' Jeff called behind him cheerily. 'Fast and st—'

'STOP!' Handsome squealed.

In front of Piggy Handsome and Jeff, a long line of traffic was trundling to a halt at a set of traffic lights.

'Oh, er, oops!' Jeff stopped flapping, but Piggy Handsome, in his runaway skate, didn't slow down one bit. So Jeff landed on the toe of the roller boot, and they hurtled onwards.

'EEEEP!'

'TWEEEET!'

The friends squeezed their eyes tight shut as they whizzed under buses and between the wheels of cars, trucks and lorries.

FYOOM! FYOOM! FYOOM!

. . . .

Six fur-frizzing seconds later, close to the top

of a hill and away from the roar of the monstrous main road, the roller boot finally came to a squeaky . . . stop.

Piggy Handsome opened his eyes, then patted his head to check it was still there.

'Cor, that was exciting!' Jeff chuckled, hopping off the skate and giving his feathers a quick fluff.

'Yes, I suppose it *was* exciting,' Piggy Handsome muttered with one eye twitching. 'If you think NEARLY GETTING SQUASHED FLATTER THAN A FRENCH CRÊPE IS EXCITING!'

'A French *what*?' Jeff looked confused.

'A pancake! A French pancake. They are flatter than normal ones. They are really, really, really, very super FLAT!'

'Nah! It was all *completely* under control,' Jeff protested as he kicked one of the wheels. 'Apart from this thing nearly falling off.'

'Where are we anyway?' Handsome spluttered, heaving himself out of the roller boot. 'I assume you do know the way to the seafront?'

'Well, the truth is,' Jeff replied, 'I've never been to the seafront. I usually stop when I get to the far end of Pickering Park. I'm more of a tree

121

bird than a seabird, if you know what I mean, and—'

'Get to the point, Jeffry!' Handsome interrupted. 'Do you know the way or don't you?'

'No. I don't actually *know* the way, but I thought . . .'

'You thought WHAT?'

Piggy Handsome smashed his own sunglasses on to the pavement. Jeff waited for him to stop stamping on them before replying, 'I thought we'd probably find the seafront if we just followed these signs.'

Jeff was pointing to an absolutely massive

black-and-white sign, which was right next to them.

SEAFRONT THIS WAY! the sign read cheerfully.

'Right. Well. Good,' Handsome mumbled. 'We'd better go then, or we'll miss the start and . . . Ooh!'

Piggy Handsome had spotted a van parked beneath some low branches in a shady clearing. It had a big plastic hotdog on top of it.

With his tummy rumbling, and a Brilliant World Record eating competition ahead of him, Piggy Handsome decided a quick snack was *just* what he needed.

Rudemption!
or There's just no forgiving bad manners

'Wait here, Jeffry,' Handsome ordered, striding off towards the hotdog van. 'I'll be back in a moment.'

'No problem!' Jeff was already busying himself fixing the wobbly wheel on the roller boot. Or at least, he was hitting it with a dusty twig.

'I say!' Piggy Handsome shouted up to the window of the hotdog van. 'I don't eat hotdogs, but I'd very much like a vegetarian bean burger, please! Brown bap. Extra ketchup. And a dollop of piccalilli, if you have any?'

Well, the humans inside the van didn't so much as glance down in Piggy Handsome's direction.

'I wanted a big, shiny, fast getaway car!' one of the humans was complaining. 'Not a bloomin' great van with a hotdog on top! We're not exactly very in-con-pixie-nuts. I mean, in-spon-tick-you-lus. I mean . . . never mind.'

'IN-CON-SPICK-YOU-US!' Handsome shouted helpfully (because he knew the word the human was trying to say was 'inconspicuous', meaning 'not drawing people's attention').

The humans carried on ignoring him.

One was busy emptying out a large grey sack. Her blue eyes bulged as rings and bracelets cascaded out of the bag like a sparkling, jingly waterfall.

The other one was gnawing on a stick of rock and counting a fat wad of money.

It was the dastardly Dixons!

The horrible robbers, counting their loot.

'Excuse me!' Piggy Handsome yelled even louder. 'EXCUSE ME!'

Nothing.

'Stop moaning, Dan, you big ninny!' Dolly said, trying on some gold earrings. 'We'll just hide here, and as soon as it's dark, we'll drive to the countryside and find a big house to live in. Then we'll hide the hotdog van, in case anyone saw us.'

'But . . . how are we gonna hide a huge van with a flippin' great hotdog on top of it?' Dan cried.

'We'll, er . . . We'll bury it.'

'Yeah! Brilliant! We'll set off tonight, but remember, I don't want to live near any cows,' Dan said. 'Their eyes are too big.'

'Or sheep,' Dolly replied. 'I hate sheep. Pass the Custard Creams.'

Outside the van, Piggy Handsome was huffing about how rude the humans were being. He very much wanted a bean burger and they were very much *not* making him one.

'I will *sell* you one Custard Cream,' Dan said, hugging the packet to his chest. 'For fifty quid!'

'Sounds like a bargain!' Dolly cackled, swiping a fifty-pound note off the big pile of cash on the counter and handing it over.

Handsome, as hungry as he was angry, climbed up on to a branch of a tree before leaping in through the open window of the van.

'I *said* I would like a bean burger,' Handsome repeated. 'Please.'

Still . . .

nothing.

Dolly was munching on her fifty-quid biscuit, still cackling. Dan was leaning over their dodgy hoard, sniggering.

'FINE!'

Oh dear. With an expression as black as a brewing thunderstorm, Piggy Handsome looked around the van for something to throw at them, then hopped to the driver's seat and kicked the handbrake once,

twice,

three times until . . .

CLUNK!

It popped and released.

The van began to roll away, the tree branches scraping noisily on its roof.

'Wha . . . ?' said Dan.

'Eh?' said Dolly.

They both turned

to see Piggy Handsome standing with his

hands on his hips (his cape billowing just a *little*)

before bounding out of the window.

Handsome watched triumphantly as the hotdog van continued rolling backwards down the hill.

'Good riddance, you ... PARSNIPS!' Handsome shouted, picking up a handful of pine cones from the ground and pelting the van with them.

'What was THAT?' Dolly yelped.

'Oh no!' Dan howled. 'They've found us, we're under attack!'

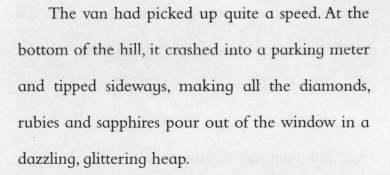

The van had picked up quite a speed. At the bottom of the hill, it crashed into a parking meter and tipped sideways, making all the diamonds, rubies and sapphires pour out of the window in a dazzling, glittering heap.

'No!' shouted Dan.

'NOOO!' shouted Dolly.

★

'What's going on down there?' Jeff asked, as he reattached his harness and Piggy returned to settle back into his roller-boot carriage.

'What's going on down there is the most dreadful customer service I have *ever* had the misfortune to come across!' Handsome replied. 'Now, Jeffry, take me to my destiny!'

Setting off once more, Piggy Handsome and Jeff paid no attention to the loud shouts coming from behind them.

And they didn't really listen to the *WOO-WOO-WOO!* of the police sirens suddenly blaring in the distance.

Because as Handsome and Jeff reached the brow of the hill, a wonderful view was suddenly laid before them. Far below, down a steep slope, was a long promenade with a big white Ferris wheel. Hundreds of people were milling about, crowding around the colourful stands selling drinks and ice creams.

And beyond the promenade, there was an

absolute whopper of an ocean, all choppy, sparkling and blue.

'I've done it, Jeffry,' Piggy Handsome whispered, his eyes as wide as bean burgers. 'I've found the seafront!'

Champtastical!
or The moment you've all been waiting for

'WHEEEEEEE!' squawked Jeff as he and Piggy Handsome freewheeled all the way down to the seafront before coming to a halt outside a sweet shop. They parked the boot and gazed around them.

The promenade was brimming with people. In every direction there were happy faces and the air was filled with the summery scents of candyfloss, suntan cream and . . . chips.

Piggy Handsome stuck his nose up and sniffed.

'This way!' he said, marching off towards a large crowd of people. Jeff hopped along behind him, ducking to avoid being whipped in the face by Handsome's cape.

As they approached the crowd, weaving their way through the humans' pink, pudgy, flip-flopped feet, a loudspeaker suddenly boomed:

'Welcome one and all to the second annual Brilliant World Record Chip Chomping Championship!

'Before this year's contestants take their places, please give a big hand for the current Brilliant World Record Holder and Chip Chomping Champ, Charlie "The Chops" Fryer!'

'Charlie! Charlie! Charlie!' the crowd chanted. As Piggy Handsome and Jeff squeezed their way to the front, an enormous human stepped forwards.

Square and rigid as a garden shed, he was wearing a blue T-shirt with 'The Chops' written across the front.

'What the lollypop is *that*?' Piggy Handsome asked.

'That's the World Champ,' Jeff tutted. 'Charlie "The Chops" Fryer is the human you have to beat.'

'No problem, Jeffry!' Handsome said confidently. Then his voice suddenly went strangely shrill. 'Look, Jeffry! LOOK! They're HERE!'

Handsome was pointing towards a group of humans who were madly scribbling things down in notepads. Next to them . . .

CLICKCLICKCLICKCLICK!

. . . more humans were snapping away with their cameras, trying to get close-ups of Charlie 'The Chops' Fryer.

And to the far side, arranging all the microphones and filming equipment, were the presenter and crew from . . .

'GIBBLESBY TV NEWS!'

Piggy Handsome's eyes were bulging with excitement.

'How do I look, Jeffry?' Handsome asked breathily. 'Is my hair all right?'

The truth was, Piggy Handsome's hair had not benefited from their chaotic journey to the seafront.

His usually perfectly coiffed quiff was now sticking out in various directions. Part of it was matted and had bits of leaf poking through.

Jeff hid one leg in his feathers. 'Your hair looks *great*,' he said. 'Now, quick, it looks like the contestants are taking their places.'

Set out in front of the news reporters and film crew was a very long table lined with chairs. Charlie 'The Chops' Fryer had already sat down in the 'No. 1' chair, and other humans (some of them doing strange stretches with their jaws) were sitting down too.

Piggy Handsome scampered down the line, looking for a place.

'Handsome!' Jeff called out. 'Don't you need to register to get a seat?' He pointed at an official sitting at a small table, tapping her red fingernails on a clipboard.

'No need!' Piggy Handsome replied. 'There's a spare seat right here! No. 12!'

Piggy Handsome leaped up on to the chair, stretched up to rest his little paws on the table, and gazed down the long line of competitors.

Jeff went and perched on some railings next to

the TV crew, to get a good view of the action.

Right at the other end of the table, a bowl of chips had been placed in front of Charlie.

'Pah!' Handsome scoffed. 'Look at it, Jeffry? Did he become a Brilliant World Record holder by eating a tiny bowl of chips like that?

Huphuphuphuphup! I'll break this record, no problem!'

'Er, actually,' Jeff said. 'It's not tiny. It's just far away.'

Handsome looked puzzled. 'What do you mean, Jeffry?'

'It's all about perspective,' Jeff explained. That is a *very large* bowl of chips, but it is *very* far away. Being far away makes it look small. But it ain't.'

Jeff was right. The bowl was actually about the size of a washing-up bowl – even bigger, perhaps. And it was piled high with a mountain of steaming chips.

'Ohhh,' Handsome said curiously as he watched one of the officials move up the line towards him handing out the chips. Each bowl that was placed on the table looked heftier than the last until, finally, an absolutely gargantuan bowl of chips was slammed down in front of Piggy Handsome with a mighty FWOMP!

'Attention, please!' the loudspeaker suddenly boomed. 'The Championship Chips have been weighed and verified by the Official Brilliant World Record Judge. Each bowl weighs precisely twelve kilograms . . .'

'You still there, Handsome?' Jeff chuckled. 'I can't see you behind those chips. You ain't worried, are you?'

Piggy Handsome *was* worried. Now, twelve kilograms was ten times more than Piggy Handsome weighed *himself* – but *that* wasn't what was worrying him.

He peeped around the gigantic bowl. 'Jeffry, I am a *little* concerned,' he said, 'because I suspect these chips have been doused with rather cheap vinegar. I could get the most dreadful heartburn and . . .'

The loudspeaker drowned him out.

'The current Brilliant World Record, held by Charlie "The Chops" Fryer, stands at ten and a half kilograms of chips chomped in three minutes. If anyone chomps more than that today, they will set a new Brilliant World Record.'

The crowd cheered and clapped and stomped their feet.

'Are the competitors ready?' the loudspeaker continued.

'Then let's begin the countdown!'

Finally, *finally*, Piggy Handsome's big moment had arrived.

10

ButtAstrophy!
or What to do when things start going pear-shaped

'Er, excuse me!' Handsome shouted, putting his hand in the air. 'May I just ask what type of vinegar you put on these chips? I'm hoping it was Italian balsamic, but it smells rather—'

'Ten . . . nine . . . eight . . .'

Of course, as was always the case, none of the humans heard Piggy Handsome. None of the humans had even noticed he was there. Handsome was barely visible to the crowd, just peeping up over the table and hidden anyway by the heap of chips in front of him.

'seven . . . six . . .'

Handsome tried again. 'Please tell me this isn't malt vinegar I can smell—'

'five . . . four . . . Oh! Our latecomer has just arrived. Please wait one moment while local great-grandma Mildred Boss takes her place!'

Piggy Handsome watched as the Mildred human slowly made her way along the table.

'Oh, hang on . . .' Jeff said, peering around the cameras to see. 'Where's she gonna sit?'

As humans go, Mildred was on the elderly side, with softly wrinkled skin, pure white hair and very thick, round glasses. The crowd muttered and nudged one other as she squeezed past the other competitors. A few of them giggled quietly. Charlie 'The Chops' Fryer laughed out loud. 'Looks like this is gonna be even easier than last year!' he roared.

Jeffry, meanwhile, was getting increasingly worried. It looked like the Mildred human was heading for Piggy Handsome's chair.

Suddenly, the railing Jeff was perched on wobbled and he found himself in shadow.

'Afternoon!' Jeff chirped to the enormous white seagull that had landed and was peering down at him. 'You here to watch the action, eh?'

'Actually,' the gull squawked sharply, 'I'm here to watch *you* . . .'

'Me?' Jeff said.

'Yes, you!' screeched a new voice from Jeff's other side. The second gull was even bigger than the first — a skanky old sack of a bird, with icy grey eyes and scraggy black wings.

Suddenly, screechy voices were coming from everywhere.

'What are you doing here?'

'Get your eyes off those chips!'

'This is our patch!'

'You don't belong here, birdie!'

'So SCRAM!'

'Er, Handsome . . .' Jeff called nervously as the gulls pushed and prodded him, and their friends circled overhead. 'I might need some help over here, pal!'

Unfortunately, just as Jeffry suspected, things were about to start going rather wrong for Piggy Handsome too. At the very moment Jeff shouted 'HELP!', Piggy Handsome also found himself suddenly in shadow.

And when he looked up to see what had blotted out the sun, he saw Mildred's very plump, wide bottom – and it was heading straight for him.

'Can't you see this seat is taken?' he shouted. 'I'm already . . . *EEEEEEPPPffttttttt!*'

If the truth be known, this was not the first time Piggy Handsome had been sat on.

That manky old moggy Cranky Scrapper frequently liked to sit on Handsome.

But Mildred was considerably heavier than Cranky – there was virtually no wriggle room.

'Gerdoff me!' Handsome gasped. '*Arfpht!* Gerdoff!'

The countdown began again.

'Ten . . . nine . . . eight . . . seven . . .'

Jeff was surrounded by hostile birds . . .

Piggy Handsome was stuck under Mildred's bottom . . .

'six . . . five . . . four . . .'

'He's come for our scraps!' squawked the seagulls.

'*Arfpht!* Gerdoff!'

'We'll show him!'

'three . . . two . . . one . . . BEGIN!'

The crowd roared as all the competitors began shovelling chips into their mouths.

'Gerdoff me, you LUMP!' Poor Handsome. He was well and truly trapped.

'HELP! Handsome, HELP!' Poor Jeff. Whichever way he fluttered, sharp beaks and beating wings were there to meet him.

'OW! TWEEET! OW! HELP!'

'Gerdoff me! Jerffry! *Arʃpht!* Jerffry!'

Anyone passing by wouldn't have noticed anything unusual about any of this. They'd have seen a bunch of gulls swooping and circling, as they tend to do – but they wouldn't have seen the tiny blue bird against the big blue sky, flitting and fluttering for all his life was worth.

And they definitely wouldn't have seen Piggy Handsome! No one would have suspected that on chair No. 12, under the fleshy buttocks of an old human called Mildred, there was a guinea pig wondering if he and his good friend Jeff would ever make it home alive.

A guinea pig who was about to have an idea – possibly the only *properly* good idea he'd ever had in his life.

You might have already guessed what Piggy Handsome's idea was. There was only one way he was going to get out from under Mildred's bottom in time to help Jeff. Handsome twisted round, opened his mouth as wide as he could and . . .

CHOMP!

. . . bit Mildred's bum.

'Owwwwwwwwwwwwwweeeeeeee!' Mildred shrieked as she shot out of her chair.

With a huge gasp of pain, Mildred sucked up all the chips in her bowl in one go. She swallowed the lot with a gulp, then sat back down in shock.

But not before Piggy Handsome had made his escape and sprung on to the table.

'Jeffry!' Handsome yelled. 'Jeffry, I'm coming!'

Piggy Handsome sprinted down the long table towards the horrible seagulls.

To human onlookers, with his cape billowing over his head, he simply looked like a used napkin, blowing along the table in the breeze.

'Stop! Leave me alone!' Jeff was pleading as he dodged the nips and jabs. The poor budgie was looking quite exhausted, like he might just drop from the sky if the gulls didn't stop soon.

Piggy Handsome skidded to a halt in front of Charlie 'The Chops' Fryer, who was still guzzling his chips.

'Leave him alone, you fiends!' Piggy Handsome yelled, shaking his fists at the seagulls . . . who paid him no attention at all.

'Fine!' Handsome screamed. 'You asked for it! There's only one thing for it!'

Well, I expect you know what's coming.

'HYAAAA-AWWW!'

Yes. Despite the fact that he wasn't even wearing his silk Kung Fu outfit, the situation seemed serious enough to whip out some of Great Uncle Chan Zen Handsome's very special Kung Fu moves.

'HAAAAR-WAH!'

If anyone in the crowd noticed that there was a guinea pig on the table, doing three roly-polys, followed by four sit-ups and a double fist pump, they didn't say so.

It's very likely that none of them *did* notice, because they all had their eyes on the big countdown clock, which was showing that there were only six seconds to go before time was up.

'Five . . . four . . . THREE . . . TWO . . .'

What happened next was . . . unexpected.

Piggy Handsome span on one heel . . .

'HYAAAA-AWWW!'

. . . and attempted a Kung Fu cartwheel. Partly helped by some chip grease on the tablecloth, his left foot made contact with Charlie's bowl, with a mighty impact.

Just as Charlie was about to try to stuff the last of his chips into his mouth, the bowl took to the air like a rocket!

'Oi!' shouted Charlie, spitting chips out at all angles.

'Oh, yes, take *that*!' shouted Handsome, as he watched the huge bowl spin through the air and up, up, up towards the ghastly gulls.

'WAARGH!' one gull cried as the bowl rebounded off his chest. All the others dived through the air to gulp the chips that were plummeting towards the sea.

Jeff seized his chance to escape. He dived down,

down, down, landed on a bin, then hid underneath a chocolate bar wrapper.

' . . . ONE!'

HVMOOOM! A klaxon hooted. The competition was over.

The crowd went completely silent, waiting for the results of the contest. The Official Judge patrolled the length of the table, marking notes on her clipboard.

'And the winner is . . .' the loudspeaker boomed, 'Mildred Boss! Our new Brilliant World Record Holder and Chip Chomping Champion!'

Piggy Handsome had hopped off the table, and scurried over to the bin where Jeff was hiding.

'Jeffry? Are you there?' he whispered, as the news reporters and photographers gathered around Mildred, shouting for her attention.

Jeff peeped out.

'Yeah, I'm here,' he said quietly. 'Maybe we could just go h—'

'Let's go home!' Handsome interrupted. 'I've had quite enough of the seafront for one day.'

11

Anonpomposity!

or The radio thingy's gonna get it

'I told you I was more of a tree bird than a seabird,'
Jeff sighed the next morning. 'Seabirds are horrible!
Tree birds just talk about twigs and stuff. They
never pull out each other's feathers and—'

FLWAT! Handsome clouted Jeff on the side of

the head with the morning newspaper.

'Ssshh!' he said. 'That's enough about you. Let's see how many pictures I'm in!'

The results of the Chip Chomping Championship had made front-page news:

SURPRISE CHIP CHOMPING VICTORY FOR GREAT GRANDMOTHER MILDRED BOSS! the headline announced.

And underneath:

> **Crowds were shocked yesterday when Charlie 'The Chops' Fryer was defeated in his attempt to break his own Brilliant**

World Record by local great-grandmother Mildred Boss.

Fryer was, in fact, disqualified from the contest when the judge noted the previous champion had – bizarrely – thrown his own bowl into the sea, meaning the total amount of chips he had chomped could not be verified.

Mildred Boss, meanwhile, was declared winner, having chomped almost her entire bowl of twelve kilograms of chips. Congratulations, Mildred! (For more pictures, turn to page four.)

Piggy Handsome flicked to page four and studied all the photographs very closely.

'Look!' he cried. 'A picture of chair No. 12!'

But all that could be seen of Handsome was a tiny hint of ear fluff poking out from behind the bowl.

'Maybe you're in this one,' Jeff said, leaning down and squinting at a picture of Charlie, taken the moment his bowl took to the air.

But the only part of Piggy Handsome showing was the pointy tip of his little toenail, mid-kung fu cartwheel.

'NOTHING!' Handsome shrieked. 'Nothing, nothing, nothing!'

'What's this?' a hoarse feline voice suddenly sneered. Cranky Scrapper had, as usual, sneaked into the room, silent and unannounced. 'Not famous yet, *little Piggy*? No one paying you any attention? Shame. I'd just give up if I were you.' She slunk away again, grinning.

It was enough to make Piggy Handsome blow his top, good and proper.

'AAAARGGGHH!'

Handsome stamped on the newspaper with his

pointy, piggy little feet. Then he picked it up and screwed it into a tight ball before chucking it as hard as he could.

It hit a button on the radio. A deep, soothing human voice floated out from the speaker.

'...eight o'clock, here are today's news headlines. A local great-grandmother, Mildred Boss, yesterday became a new Brilliant World Record holder . . .'

'What am I to do now, Jeffry?' Handsome wailed, as he gazed at the portraits of his grand and extremely famous ancestors. 'Is Cranky right? Can this *really* be all there is for me?'

'Listen, Handsome,' Jeff said softly. 'I know you didn't break a Brilliant World Record, and you still ain't got your picture in the paper, but you still did something special yesterday, you know.'

'Did I?' Handsome sighed.

'Course you did!' Jeff chuckled. 'Handsome, you *saved* me . . .'

'Ssshh!'

'You saved my lif—'

'SSSSHHHHH, Jeffry! Listen!'

'. . . led to the capture of the hotdog van villains, Dan and Dolly Dixon. The pair had robbed Jones's

Jewellery Shop, taking six hundred thousand pounds' worth of jewels and cash, but they were arrested when they lost control of their getaway hotdog van, and it crashed into a parking meter at the bottom of Seaview Hill.'

Piggy Handsome gasped.

The radio voice continued:

'An eyewitness told Gibblesby FM that it was no mistake the thieves were caught. Let's speak to the arresting officer, Constable Shift.

'Constable, what do you believe led to the arrest of Dan and Dolly Dixon?'

'Good morning, Ann. Well, the robbers weren't making much sense, but they insisted they had come under attack at the top of the hill, before the van lost control. In fact, the police didn't arrive until several minutes later. We suspect that, somewhere out there, is a *hero* . . .'

'That's me!' Piggy Handsome whispered.

'. . . but clearly, he or she is a hero who wishes to remain anonymous . . .'

'NO, I DON'T!' Handsome yelled.

'. . .someone who doesn't want to put themselves in the spotlight . . .'

182

'YES, I DO!'

'But we hope that hero is listening now. And if you are, Gibblesby Police Force thanks you.'

'IT WAS ME! IT WAS ME!' Handsome shouted. 'Why aren't you listening? Jeffry, why aren't they listening?'

One eye started twitching. Trembling with rage, Handsome shook the radio violently, then twirled the knob, making the volume go up and down.

'Handsome, they can't hear you 'cos that's not a telephone,' Jeff said, shaking his head. 'It's a radio and—'

'Listen to me!' Handsome shouted at the radio again. 'My name is Piggy Handsome! I am the hero! *I even have a cape!* It's me! Me! You . . . stupid . . . *radio thingy*!'

Piggy Handsome kicked the radio right in the speaker . . .

RASSSSP!

Then he grabbed a floppy cabbage from his dining table and slapped the radio with it . . .

'You . . . PARSNIPS!'

. . . over and over again.

Jeff Budgie rolled his eyes, chuckled, and

fluttered to his perch.

He stuck one leg in his feathers.

And closed his eyes for a snooze.

The End

And so, Piggy Handsome will stay in a tizz,

Enraged the world STILL doesn't know who he is!

Yes, poor Piggy Handsome. He thought he'd go far.

But he'll never give up! Not until he's a STAR!

187